10/92

RAPUNZEL

FROM THE **BROTHERS GRIMM**

Illustrated by **CAROL HEYER**

Ideals Children's Books · Nashville, Tennessee

Published by Ideals Publishing Corporation
Nashville, Tennessee 37210

Printed and bound in Mexico.

Library of Congress Cataloging-in-Publication Data

Rapunzel. English
Rapunzel/illustrated by Carol Heyer.
p.   cm.
Summary: A beautiful girl with extraordinarily long golden hair
is imprisoned in a lonely tower by a witch.
ISBN 0-8249-8585-0 (lib. bdg.)—ISBN 0-8249-8558-3 (trade)
[1. Fairy tales. 2. Folklore—Germany.] I. Heyer, Carol, 1950- ill.
II. Title.
PZ8.R1866   1992
398.21—dc20   92-6712
                                                CIP
                                                AC

The illustrations in this book are rendered in acrylic on
canvas using live models.
The display type is set in Cloister Initials.
The text type is set in Sabon.
Color separations were made by Rayson Films, Inc.,
Waukesha, Wisconsin.
Printed and bound by R.R. Donnelley & Sons.

Designed by Joy Chu.

THIS BOOK IS DEDICATED TO MY FATHER AND MENTOR,
WILLIAM JEROME HEYER, WITH ALL OF MY
APPRECIATION AND LOVE, ALWAYS.

                                                – C.H.

SPECIAL THANKS TO MODELS:
GABY SALICK...RAPUNZEL
SUSAN DAVIS ATKINSON ....THE WITCH GOTHEL
JEFF HOOVER ....THE PRINCE
MARSHA HAIK ....THE MOTHER
PHILIP HAIK ....THE FATHER
JESSICA HAIK..................................BABY RAPUNZEL
WILLIAM JEROME HEYER ....THE KING
MERLYN HUTSON HEYER ....THE QUEEN

There once lived a man and a woman who had long wished for a child of their own.

After many years had passed, the couple's wish was finally to be granted. They waited happily through the winter and the spring for the arrival of their child.

At the back of their home, a little window overlooked a high wall surrounding a garden filled with the finest vegetables and flowers. No one dared venture into this garden, for it belonged to a witch so powerful that all the world feared her.

One day, the woman stood at her window, looking into the witch's garden, and she noticed a patch of the finest rampion. The green leaves looked so fresh and tender that she began to wish for some, and at length she longed for them greatly.

The wife's desire for the vegetable increased for many days. She soon began to pine away, growing more pale and miserable as time went by.

Her husband became worried.

"What is the matter, dear wife?" he asked.

"Oh," she answered mournfully, "I shall surely die unless I eat some rampion from old Gothel's garden."

The man loved his wife very much, and he thought
to himself, *Rather than lose my dearest love, I will get
some of that rampion, cost whatever it will.*

So in the twilight, he climbed over the wall and into
the witch's garden. He hastily plucked a handful of
rampion and took it home to his wife.

At once, the woman made a salad with the greens
and then ate to her heart's content. It tasted so good and
she liked it so much that the next day she longed for the
rampion three times as much as before.

So again the husband went into the early twilight, but just as he started back toward home, he saw the witch standing before him.

"How dare you climb into my garden like a thief and steal my rampion!" Gothel bellowed, her eyes flashing in anger. "You shall pay for this!"

"Oh, please," he begged, "be merciful rather than just, my neighbor. I have stolen your food only through necessity. My wife saw your rampion from her window and became so possessed with longing for it that she would have died without it."

Then the witch replied, "If this is true, you may have all the rampion that you desire, but you and your wife shall both pay. When your baby is born, you must give it to me. All will go well with the child, and I will care for it like a mother."

In his fear, the man promised, and at the sound of the baby's first cry, Gothel appeared. Giving the child the name of Rapunzel, which means rampion, the old witch took the newborn girl away.

Rapunzel grew to become the most beautiful child in the world. But when the girl reached the age of twelve, the witch took her into the middle of the woods and shut her up in a tower which had neither steps nor door and only a small window above.

When Gothel wanted to visit the child, she would stand beneath the tower window and cry, "Rapunzel, Rapunzel! Let down your hair!"

Rapunzel's beautiful long hair shone like gold. Whenever she heard the witch's call, Rapunzel opened the window and let her silky braid fall below. Then the witch held fast to the long hair, as though it were a rope, and scaled the tower wall.

The years passed away as Rapunzel tried to ease her loneliness by listening to the birds and singing her own sweet songs. The old witch was her only companion.

One day, it happened that the king's son came riding through the woods. As the prince drew near the tower, he heard singing so lovely that he stood still and listened.

Wishing to go inside, the king's son sought a door in the tower, yet he found none.

Giving up, the prince rode home, but Rapunzel's voice had entered his heart, and every day, he went back into the woods to hear her songs. Once, as he stood hidden behind a tree, he saw the old witch approaching, and he listened quietly while she called, "O Rapunzel, Rapunzel! Let down your hair."

Then the prince saw the shimmering tress spill from above and how the witch clambered up to the window. He said to himself, "Since that is the ladder, I will climb it and seek my fortune."

On the next day, as soon as it began to grow dark, the prince drew near the tower and cried, "O Rapunzel, Rapunzel! Let down your hair."

The hair came tumbling out, and up he climbed.

Rapunzel drew back in terror as his face appeared in her window, for she had never seen a man. But the king's son was a gentle soul. He spoke kindly to Rapunzel of how her singing had so filled his heart that he could have no peace until he had seen her for himself.

His words so soothed Rapunzel that she soon forgot to be afraid. And when he asked if she would take him for her husband, she thought, *I like him much better than old Mother Gothel—he is so young and kind.* She gently placed her hand in his.

"I would willingly go with you," she answered, "but I cannot get out of this tower. When you come to see me, if you will bring each time a silken rope, I will make a ladder. When it is long enough, I will get down by it, and you may take me away on your horse."

They agreed that he should visit only in the evening to avoid old Gothel, who always came in the daytime.

The witch knew nothing of what had passed until one day when Rapunzel accidentally asked, "Mother Gothel, why is it that you climb up here so slowly, but the prince is with me in only a moment?"

"O wicked child," cried the witch, "what is this I hear? I thought I had hidden you from all the world, and still you have betrayed me!"

In her anger, Gothel seized Rapunzel's beautiful hair with her left hand and grasped a pair of shears with her right—snip, snap—the beautiful locks fell to the floor in a golden heap.

Then the old hag took Rapunzel to a faraway, deserted wasteland and abandoned her there to live a life of great woe and misery.

The witch returned to the tower early that evening
and fastened the severed locks of hair to the window.
She waited patiently until the king's son appeared.

"Rapunzel, Rapunzel! Let down your hair," he cried.

Gothel dropped the hair down, and the prince
climbed up—but instead of his dear Rapunzel, he found

the evil witch glaring at him with wicked, glittering eyes.

"Aha!" she screeched, mocking him. "You came for your darling, but the sweet bird sits no longer in the nest, and she sings no more. The cat has got her and will now scratch out your eyes! Rapunzel is lost to you, and you shall see her no more."

The prince felt his heart breaking with grief. In his agony, he sprang from the tower, escaping the fall with life, but blinded by the thorn bushes on which he landed.

He stumbled sightlessly throughout the woods, eating only roots and berries, lamenting and weeping for the loss of his dearest Rapunzel.

And so he wandered for several years until, at last, he came to the wasteland where his true love lived.

The blinded prince heard a soft song that he thought
he knew, and when he drew close to the source of the
familiar sound, Rapunzel knew him. She fell against
him, weeping, and when her tears touched his eyes, they
became clear again—he could see as well as ever.

Clasping her hand in his, the prince led Rapunzel away
to his kingdom. And there in the castle they lived long lives
together, filled with happiness and delight.